For Clappy

Published in the United States of America in 2001 by MONDO
Publishing.

First published in the United Kingdom by Random House Children's
Books, 1999.

Copyright © 1999 by Ant Parker.

For information, contact:
MONDO Publishing
980 Avenue of the Americas
New York, New York 10018

Visit our web site at http://www.mondopub.com

Printed in Hong Kong.
First Mondo Printing, July 2001
01 02 03 04 05 06 07   9 8 7 6 5 4 3 2 1

ISBN 1-58653-853-5

Designed by David Neuhaus/NeuStudio, Inc.

Library of Congress Cataloging-in-Publication Data available
upon request.

Wake Up, Ginger

Ant Parker

MONDO

Ginger is asleep in his box.

"Here I am, Ginger..."

"You can't catch me!"

"Here I am, Ginger..."

"Here I am, Ginger..."

"Here I am, Ginger..."

"You can't catch me!"

"Here I am, Ginger..."

"Here I am, Ginger..."

"Go back to sleep, Ginger..."

"You'll *never* catch me!"